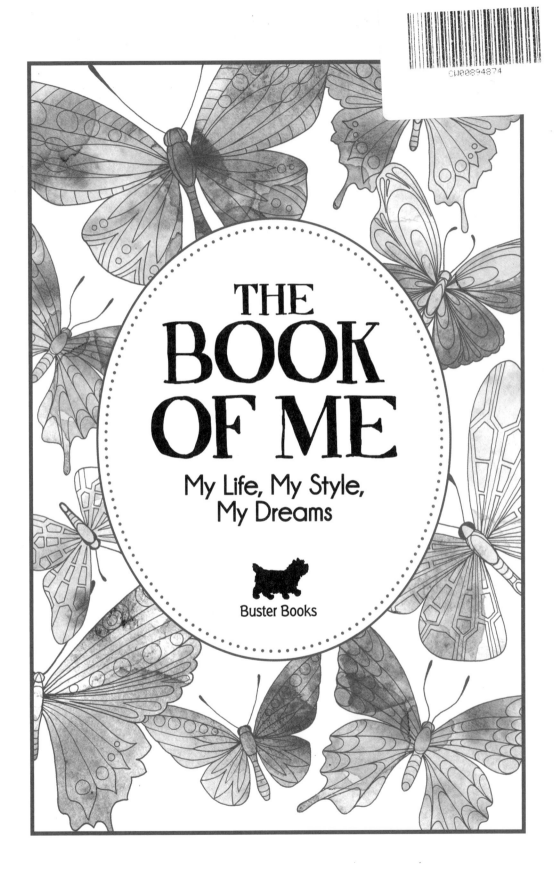

THE BOOK OF ME

My Life, My Style, My Dreams

Buster Books

WRITTEN BY IMOGEN WILLIAMS AND ELLEN BAILEY

ILLUSTRATED BY CHELLIE CARROLL

EDITED BY IMOGEN WILLIAMS
DESIGNED BY ZOE BRADLEY
COVER DESIGN BY ANGIE ALLISON

Internet Safety:
Always ask an adult's permission before using the
internet. Never give out or post personal information,
such as your name, address or telephone number.
If a website asks you to type in your email address,
always check with an adult first.

This book was first published in Great Britain in 2017 by Buster Books,
an imprint of Michael O'Mara Books Limited,
9 Lion Yard, Tremadoc Road,
London SW4 7NQ

 www.mombooks.com/buster   Buster Books   @BusterBooks

ISBN: 978-1-78055-471-6

4 6 8 10 9 7 5

This book was printed in June 2018 by Shenzhen Wing King Tong Paper Products Co. Ltd.,
Shenzhen, Guangdong, China.

CONTENTS

GETTING STARTED

This book has been created just for you. Inside, you'll find tons of questionnaires, quizzes and top tips to answer, fill in and dream about. There is plenty of space for you to write all about yourself so you can look back and remember everything in years to come.

You can complete the book in any order you want, just look at the contents pages to choose what you want to do. Some pages have space for you to fill in the exact date, time and place, so you'll never forget exactly where you were when you completed a section. There are pages with lots of lovely quotes to motivate and inspire you. When you reach a picture, you can colour it in to really make your mark on this book that is ALL ABOUT YOU ...

THIS BOOK WAS COMPLETED BY

Natalie .R

MY FACT FILE

My name is ...Natalie..R...

My friends call me ......Nat....Cat...

I am currently ....9........................ years old.

The date today is ......6th....of.......August............................

I was born on ......31st........July........2013...

The place I was born is called ......Sydney..

My star sign is ......Leo..

I live in ...... scotland dundee braghty ferry

My current location is ...... scotland

My parents are called ...... vicky & sweyn

My best friend is called ......

My favourite TV show is ...... bued hous

My favourite colour is ...... lille

My favourite animal is ...... dogs

Dream
Big
Shine
Bright

AIM HIGH

USE THIS SPACE TO DOCUMENT ALL YOUR WILDEST WISHES. THERE IS PLENTY OF SPACE TO ADD ANY OTHER THINGS YOU WANT TO ACHIEVE.

☆ When I grow up I want to live in ...... a house ....

☆ After I finish school I want to ...... have 11 dogs ....

☆ I would like to go on holiday to ...... hawaii ....

☆ My dream job is ...... dog person ....

☆ ....

☆ ....

☆ ....

☆ ....

☆ ....

☆ ....

☆ ....

☆ ....

BOOKWORM

IF YOU COULD WRITE YOUR OWN BOOK, WHAT WOULD YOU WRITE ABOUT?
YOU COULD WRITE ABOUT YOURSELF IN AN AUTOBIOGRAPHY
OR MAKE UP A FAIRYTALE, OR PERHAPS CREATE A
TIME-TRAVEL ADVENTURE OR A MURDER MYSTERY ...
WRITE DOWN YOUR IDEAS HERE.

DESIGN YOUR BOOK COVER HERE:

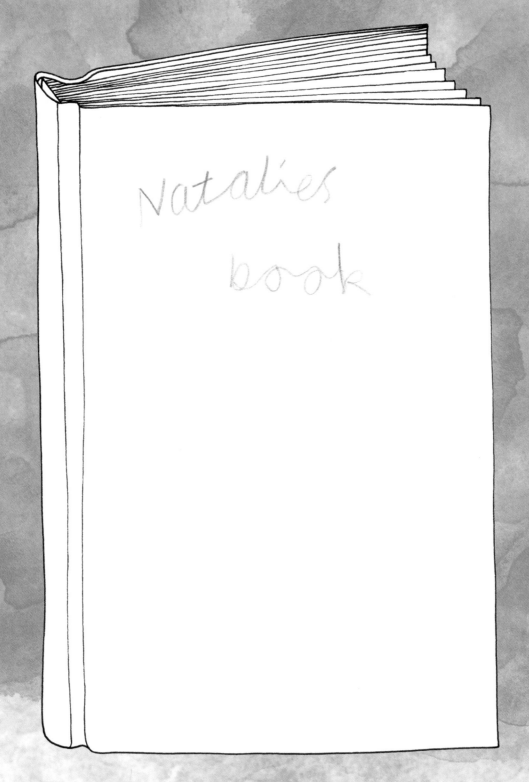

Natalies

book

FASHION WISH LIST

MAKE A LIST OF YOUR DREAM WARDROBE, FROM DESIGNER
DRESSES TO COOL COATS AND STYLISH SUNGLASSES.

♡ ....

♡ ....

♡ ....

♡ ....

♡ ....

♡ ....

♡ ....

♡ ....

♡ ....

♡ ....

♡ ....

♡ ....

WHaT'S YOUr STYLe?

Yes

Are you always on the lookout for new clothes to buy?

No

Over half an hour

START HEre

How long do you spend getting ready?

Yes, always

Under half an hour

Do you like to read fashion magazines?

Not really

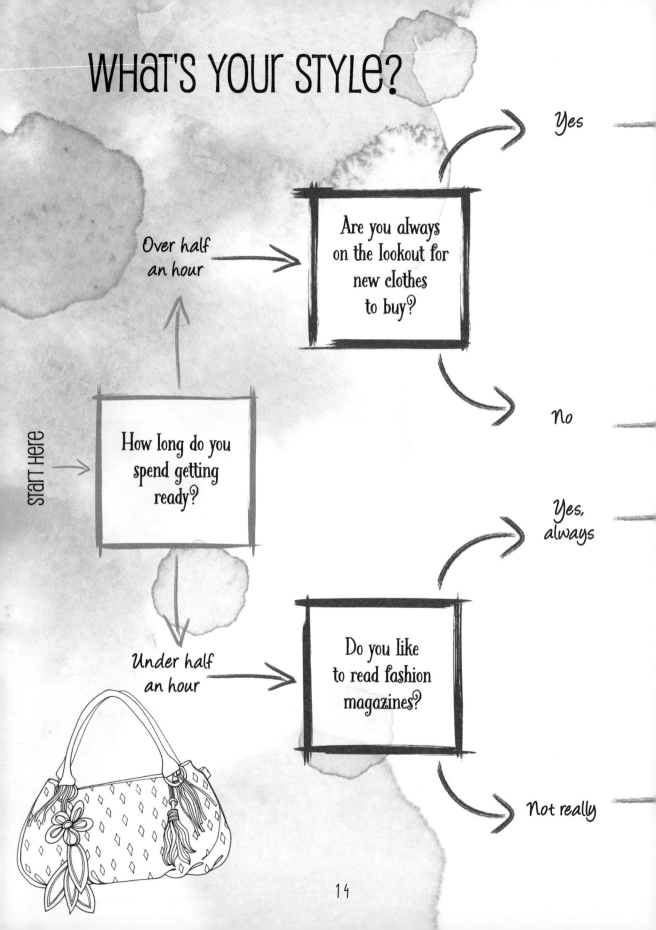

Are you up-to-date with all the latest fashion trends?

Not really, I prefer to keep my style classic and stick to what I know

Chic
Classic and timeless is your motto so your style never goes out of fashion.

Yes, and I always try out the new trends

Flamboyant
You love to try new styles and aren't afraid of wearing something bold and eye-catching.

Do you upcycle your clothes and add accessories?

Yes, it's all about being creative with fashion and style

No, I like to keep it simple

Bohemian
You like to go with the flow and aren't worried about designer labels.

I don't really care if they're practical, I just throw anything on

Do you wear clothes that are practical?

Yes, I like my clothes to be functional

Casual
You don't mind what you wear as long as it's comfortable and practical.

Dream Journal

USE THE SPACE BELOW TO DOCUMENT ONE OF YOUR DREAMS.

Date .... Time .... Place ....

What happened in your dream? ....

....

....

....

....

....

....

....

....

Have you ever had this dream before?   YES   NO

Would you like to have this dream again?   YES   NO

WHAT KIND OF DREAM WAS IT?

HAPPY   SAD   NIGHTMARE   WEIRD   BORING

Was anyone you know in your dream?   YES   NO

If yes, who? ....

....

....

....

WHICH OF THE FOLLOWING APPLY TO YOUR DREAM?
CIRCLE AS MANY AS YOU WANT.

SIGNIFICANT   INSIGNIFICANT   TOTALLY RANDOM

CONFUSING   ROMANTIC   GROSS   FUNNY

Can you think of anything that happened in real life that may explain

why you had this dream? ....

....

....

....

BEST FRIENDS QUIZ

grab your best friend and ask each other these questions to find out how well you really know one another.

Write the name of your best friend here: ....

NOW, LET THE QUESTIONS BEGIN ...

What is my middle name?

Me: ....

BFF: ....

When did we first meet?

Me: ....

BFF: ....

How long have we been friends?

Me: ....

BFF: ....

What is my favourite colour?

Me: ....

BFF: ....

Who is my celebrity crush?

Me: ....

BFF: ....

Would I rather get a takeaway or go to a restaurant?

Me: ....

BFF: ....

Do I prefer fizzy drinks or healthy smoothies?

Me: ....

BFF: ....

What is my all-time favourite film?

Me: ....

BFF: ....

Do I prefer to chat on the phone or text?

Me: ....

BFF: ....

Would I rather wear trousers or dresses for the rest of my life?

Me: ....

BFF: ....

What is my favourite way to spend a Saturday night?

Me: ....

BFF: ....

Now you can discuss each answer and record how many questions you and your best friend got right here:

My score:

/11

My BFF's score:

/11

DESIGN YOUR OWN NAIL VARNISH BOTTLES

BEAUTY WISH LIST

MAKE A LIST OF ALL THE DREAM BEAUTY PRODUCTS THAT YOU WOULD LOVE TO OWN, FROM PERFUMES AND LIP GLOSS TO BUBBLE BATH AND MAKE-UP BRUSHES.

☆ ....

☆ ....

☆ ....

☆ ....

☆ ....

☆ ....

☆ ....

☆ ....

☆ ....

☆ ....

☆ ....

☆ ....

Look up to the STARS and follow your DREAMS

INSPIRATIONAL PEOPLE

USE THE SPACE BELOW TO WRITE DOWN ALL THE PEOPLE WHO INSPIRE YOU AND WHY. THINK ABOUT PEOPLE WHO HAVE INSPIRED YOU IN THE PAST AND ALSO PEOPLE WHO YOU LOOK UP TO NOW. IT COULD BE ANYONE, FROM A TEACHER OR FAMILY MEMBER TO A CELEBRITY.

Name	Reason

INTERIOR DESIGNER

Have you ever wanted to completely redesign your bedroom? Well now you can! Answer the questions below to create the bedroom of your dreams.

What colour is your room now? ....

....

What colour would you paint your room if you could change it? ....

....

Would you change your curtains or blinds? ....

....

Would you want to move your furniture around? Where would you move it?

....

....

Would you get any new furniture in your room? ....

....

....

....

WHAT KIND OF BED DO YOU REALLY WANT?

SINGLE BED   DOUBLE BED   CABIN BED   BUNK BED

WHICH OF THE FOLLOWING WOULD YOU LIKE TO HAVE IN YOUR ROOM? CIRCLE AS MANY AS YOU WANT.

FAIRY LIGHTS   DESK   BOOKSHELVES

WALL STICKERS   SCATTER CUSHIONS   TELEVISION

BEAN BAGS   WALK-IN WARDROBE   SECRET DOOR

ARMCHAIR   PICTURES ON THE WALL   LAVA LAMP

Use the space below to write about anything else you would do.

....

....

....

....

....

....

relaxation ready

everyone can feel stressed sometimes. Here are some
tips for how you can de-stress and stay calm and relaxed.
remember, everyone is different, so there is space at the end
to add in anything that helps you stay relaxed.

☆ Have a pamper evening. You could invite a friend round or just have some
time to yourself. Don't forget the face masks!

☆ Make yourself a big mug of hot chocolate and get yourself some treats to snack on.

☆ Why not have a bath and get an early night. Lavender scented bubbles will
help you relax.

☆ Listen to some relaxing music.

☆ Spend some time doing what you love. It might be reading or writing, watching
a film or getting a coffee with friends. It's up to you.

☆ Make sure you have someone to talk to, whether it's your BFF, a family member or even a teacher.

☆ You could hit the shops with your friends for some retail therapy.

☆ Try doing some exercise. Gentle exercise like swimming can be calming, or going for a run or brisk walk around the park can help to focus your mind.

☆ ....

☆ ....

☆ ....

☆ ....

☆ ....

☆ ....

☆ ....

☆ ....

☆ ....

MY BRILLIANT BIRTHDAY

YOU CAN USE THESE PAGES TO WRITE ALL ABOUT YOUR BIRTHDAY. HOW OLD ARE YOU NOW? WHAT PRESENTS DID YOU GET? ARE YOU HAVING A PARTY?

Date .... Time .... Place ....

....

....

....

....

....

....

....

....

....

SHH, DON'T TELL ...

Make a list below of all your guilty pleasures, from cheesy music to double-chocolate chip cookies.

♡ ....

♡ ....

♡ ....

♡ ....

♡ ....

♡ ....

♡ ....

♡ ....

♡ ....

♡ ....

♡ ....

SLUMBER PARTY

FIND OUT HOW TO HAVE THE BEST EVER SLEEPOVER WITH YOUR FRIENDS.
THEN TURN THE PAGE AND USE THE SPACE TO PLAN
YOUR OWN SUPER SLUMBER PARTY.

☆ First things first, you need to decide who to invite. If you have time, you could even make invitations for your friends.

☆ Decorate your room with fairy lights and gather lots of cushions and blankets to spread around.

☆ Prepare some fun games to start the night off with. You could play 'Would You Rather', 'Charades' or 'Truth or Dare'.

☆ Have a theme. Why not give your friends a fancy-dress theme to make things more interesting.

☆ Order takeaway pizzas.

☆ Why not do some baking together and make cupcakes.
   Make sure you have lots of sprinkles to decorate them with.

☆ Plan in advance and buy some face masks, or even better, look up
   a recipe and make your own.

☆ Make sure you have your all-time favourite DVDs ready to watch.

☆ Set up the ultimate hot chocolate and snack station. Be sure to have
   marshmallows, popcorn and chocolate at the ready.

☆ And finally, don't forget to ask your friends to bring sleeping bags,
   otherwise they aren't going to get much sleep!

MY SUPER SLUMBER PARTY

PLAN YOUR PERFECT SLEEPOVER PARTY BELOW.
YOU CAN USE PAGES 32 & 33
FOR INSPIRATION.

❀ ....

❀ ....

❀ ....

❀ ....

❀ ....

❀ ....

❀ ....

❀ ....

❀ ....

❀ ....

❀ ....

❀ ....

DESIGN YOUR
OWN LIPSTICKS

MY FAVOURITE MEMORIES

WRITE DOWN SOME OF YOUR BEST MEMORIES BELOW.
WHY NOT LOOK AT OLD PHOTOS OR ASK YOUR FAMILY
TO MAKE SURE YOU DON'T FORGET ANYTHING.

♡ ....

....

....

♡ ....

....

....

♡ ....

....

....

♡ ....

....

....

♡ ....

....

....

♡ ....

....

....

♡ ....

....

....

♡ ....

....

....

♡ ....

....

....

Be strong
Be brave
Be kind

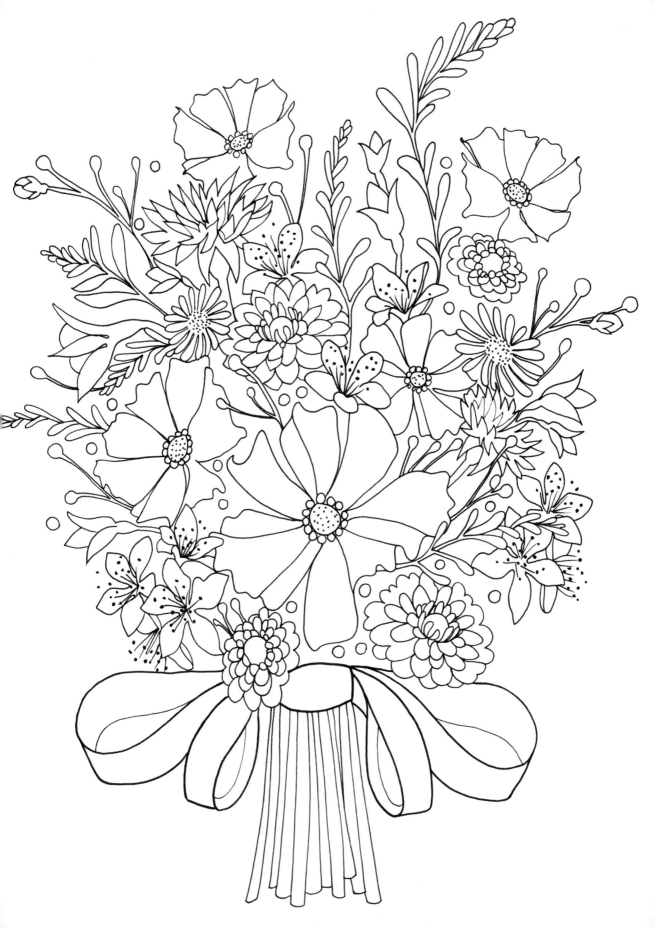

SO STYLISH

IT CAN BE HARD TO FIND YOUR STYLE OR DECIDE WHAT CLOTHES TO BUY, SO LOOK THROUGH THESE TIPS TO GIVE YOU A HELPING HAND. REMEMBER, YOU CAN WEAR ANYTHING YOU WANT. AS LONG AS YOU FEEL COMFORTABLE AND CONFIDENT, YOU WILL LOOK FABULOUS!

RECYCLE

Buy clothes that you can wear all year round. For example, you can pair a pretty dress with boots, a scarf and a pea coat for winter and in the summer you can wear the same dress with sandals and sunglasses.

ACCESSORIZE

You can change an outfit by adding simple accessories. A blouse and jeans can be glammed up with some sparkly earrings. You could even go for a professional look by pairing the outfit with a smart handbag or create the perfect casual weekend outfit with a cute hairband and trainers.

CUSTOMIZE

There are lots of things you can do to customize your wardrobe. Buy iron-on patches to adorn an old jacket, bag charms to revamp an old bag or snap some pretty clip-on earrings on to ballet pumps for an instant update.

INVEST

It's always best to invest in some classic items of clothing that you will wear a lot. A good pair of jeans, a quality coat and a leather handbag will last a long time, and then you can wear them with cheaper T-shirts and jumpers and still feel great.

MY STYLE

USE THIS SPACE TO WRITE DOWN HOW YOU THINK YOU COULD REVAMP YOUR WARDROBE, OR MAKE A LIST OF THINGS YOU WANT TO BUY.

DESIGN YOUR OWN
PERFUME BOTTLES

FAN CLUB

LIST ALL YOUR FAVOURITE CELEBRITIES BELOW,
FROM VLOGGERS TO POP STARS.

❀ ....

❀ ....

❀ ....

❀ ....

❀ ....

❀ ....

❀ ....

❀ ....

❀ ....

❀ ....

❀ ....

THE
BOOK
OF ME
My Life, My Style,
My Dreams

MY FAVOURITE BOOKS

HERE YOU CAN LIST ALL YOUR FAVOURITE BOOKS
AND WRITE DOWN WHY YOU LOVE EACH ONE.
GIVE EACH ONE A SCORE OUT OF TEN.

Book: ....

Reasons I love it: ....

....

....

score: / 10

Book: ....

Reasons I love it: ....

....

....

score: / 10

Book: ....

Reasons I love it: ....

....

....

score: / 10

Book: ....

Reasons I love it: ....

....

....

score: / 10

Book: ....

Reasons I love it: ....

....

....

score: / 10

Book: ....

Reasons I love it: ....

....

....

score: / 10

Book: ....

Reasons I love it: ....

....

....

score: / 10

personality secrets

read all about these characteristics to discover your secret personality traits.

SLEEPING POSITIONS

☆ If you lie flat on your back with your arms by your sides, you sleep in the **soldier** position. You are sensitive and thoughtful and you appreciate time alone. You have high standards, but remember to relax sometimes.

☆ If you sleep on one side, curled up with your knees bent, you sleep in the **foetal** position. You might seem shy at first, but once you feel comfortable, you are caring and generous, with a big heart.

☆ If you sleep on your front with your head turned to the side, you sleep in the **freefaller** position. You are energetic and emotional. You are a social butterfly and have lots of friends.

FINGER LENGTH

☆ If your **ring finger** is longer than your index finger, you are confident and charming.

☆ If your **index finger** is longer than your ring finger, you are a natural leader, who is considerate and sensible.

☆ If your index finger and ring finger are the **same length**, you are peaceful and warm, and always willing to listen to your friends.

Handwriting Style

☆ If you have **large** handwriting, you are outgoing and sociable. If you have **small** handwriting, you might be more timid and thoughtful.

☆ If your handwriting leans to the right, *like this*, you are friendly, kind and generous.

☆ If your handwriting stands straight up, **like this**, you are very logical and sensible.

☆ If your handwriting leans to the left, **like this**, you are quiet and keep to yourself.

Body Language

☆ Crossed arms and legs mean you are closed off and not engaging with whoever you are talking to. Try to keep your hands on your lap and uncross your legs.

☆ Slouching may suggest you look like you are disinterested and bored, not to mention it's bad for your back, so avoid this if you can.

☆ Avoiding eye contact could mean you are nervous or trying to hide something. It's good to try and maintain eye contact throughout a conversation.

☆ Weak handshakes make you seem nervous, but strong handshakes make you appear too confident. Aim for somewhere in the middle.

Dream Jobs

THINK OF YOUR TOP FIVE JOBS AND WRITE ABOUT THEM IN THE SPACE BELOW.

1. Job title: ....

Best thing about the job: ....

2. Job title: ....

Best thing about the job: ....

3. Job title: ....

Best thing about the job: ....

4. Job title: ....

Best thing about the job: ....

5. Job title: ....

Best thing about the job: ....

WRITTEN IN THE STARS

aries

Confident and enthusiastic, you throw yourself
into every opportunity and love to socialize.
You can be impatient, but that is only because
you're always on the lookout for the next big thing.

Taurus

You are patient and reliable, which makes you a
great friend. Sometimes you can be overprotective
of your loved ones, but this is only because
you really care about them.

GEMINI

You are gentle, affectionate and always
curious. Sometimes you might be indecisive, but
only because you want to experience everything
and can't decide what to do first.

cancer

Imaginative and emotional, you are a sympathetic and loyal friend. You might feel insecure occasionally, but try not to worry – your friends love you for who you are.

leo

Passionate, creative and funny, you will attract lots of friends who enjoy your lively conversations. Sometimes you might overshadow quieter members of the group, so remember to let everyone join in.

virgo

You are loyal and hard-working, and your kindness is greatly appreciated by your friends and family. You can be quite critical but try not to worry about things that you can't control.

Libra

Peaceful and gracious, you love to be surrounded
by beautiful art and music. You prefer not to be
alone, but remember that time to yourself
can be important sometimes.

Scorpio

You are passionate and decisive, which makes
you a good leader and loyal friend. You are
very secretive, which means your friends trust you,
but remember you can share your own secrets
with friends as well.

Sagittarius

Enthusiastic, curious and energetic, you have
an open mind and are always keen to explore.
You are always optimistic, but make sure you don't
push yourself to do more than you can cope with.

capricorn

You are responsible, practical and disciplined,
which means you will be a great leader. Although
you might think your way is best, remember to
let others do things their own way too.

aquarius

You are independent and energetic, but you
can also be quiet and shy in new surroundings.
You are a good listener, which your
friends will really appreciate.

pisces

Pisces are compassionate, friendly and always
willing to help others. Sometimes you may
be too trusting, but this is only because
of your generous and caring nature.

WOULD YOU raTHer ...

... only eat crisps for the rest of your life
OR never eat pizza again?

... whisper for the rest of your life OR shout for the rest of your life?

... be really tall OR really small?

... be able to speak every language in the world
OR play every instrument in the world?

... live in space OR live under the sea?

... never wash your hair again OR never wash your clothes again?

... read the book OR watch the film?

... be able to fly OR be able to read minds?

... be too hot OR too cold?

... sunbathe OR ski?

... live without music OR live without films?

... have a nice house OR have a nice car?

... have an elephant trunk OR a squirrel tail?

... have a shower OR have a bath?

... sneeze spaghetti OR cough bubbles?

... be a dog OR a cat?

YOUR PERFECT EVENING

START HERE →

Are you in the mood for an adventure or ready to relax?

It's adventure time! →

Are you ready to make lots of friends or would you rather be with your besties?

→ Let's make lots of friends

→ Besties tonight

I'm relaxation ready →

Would you rather put in loads of effort or not much at all?

→ Not much at all

→ Loads of effort

Are you in the mood to dance or would you rather have fun with your imagination?

Dancing please →

Party Time
Dust off your party shoes - it's time to go dancing!

Imagination all the way →

How late do you want to stay up?

Super-late →

Sleepover
A late night with your best friends.

I'll be ready to snuggle down in my bed soon →

Movie Night
Put your feet up and chill with friends and a good film.

How relaxed would you like to be?

A little bit →

Very →

Pamper Time
Time to rest up and relax with a face mask and bubble bath.

It's all about me tonight →

Are you ready for 'me time' or in the mood to share your evening?

I'm in the mood to kick back with friends →

Board Games Night
A fun evening at home with your friends.

QUESTION TIME

FIND A FRIEND OR FAMILY MEMBER WHO YOU WANT TO KNOW MORE ABOUT AND ASK THEM THE FOLLOWING QUESTIONS. EVERYTHING YOU'VE EVER WANTED TO KNOW IS ABOUT TO BE REVEALED ...

Date .... Time .... Place ....

Q. What is your full name? ....

....

Q. When and where were you born? ....

....

Q. Where did you grow up? ....

....

Q. What is your first memory of me? ....

....

Q. What is your dream job? ....

....

Q. What is your favourite thing to do in your spare time? ....

....

Q. If you could change one thing about yourself, what would it be? ....

....

Q. Would you rather have a cat or a dog? ....

....

Q. What is your most treasured possession? ....

....

Q. If you could live anywhere in the world, where would it be? ....

....

Q. What is your worst fear? ....

....

Q. What are you most proud of? ....

....

party planner

USE THIS SPACE TO PLAN THE PARTY OF YOUR DREAMS.

How many people would you want to invite? ....

....

....

Where would the party be? ....

....

....

Would you have a dress code? ....

....

....

Would you have a colour scheme? If so, what would it be? ....

....

....

What food would you have? It could be a three course meal or just canapés.

....

....

....

What entertainment would you have? Do you have any friends who are in a band or dance group who could perform? ....

....

....

What would you wear to the party if you could choose anything you wanted?

....

....

....

If you could give each guest a goodie bag at the end of the night, what would

you put in it? ....

....

....

Jot down anything else you would do here: ....

....

....

....

....

....

a Day IN MY LIFE ...

answer the questions below about a typical day in your life
for you to look back at and remember in years to come.

Date .... Time .... Place ....

What time did you wake up? ....
....

Did you make your bed? ....
....

Did you have a shower or a bath? ....
....

What are you wearing today? ....
....

What did you have for breakfast? ....
....

What did you do today? ....
....

Have you watched any television today? If so, what did you watch?

....

....

If you could have done absolutely anything you wanted today, what would it

have been? ....

....

What was the most boring thing you did today? ....

....

....

What was the most exciting thing about today? ....

....

....

Has anyone made you laugh today? ....

....

STYLISH SHOES

It's time to design your own shoes. Add doodles and patterns to these shoes to give them your own unique style and then colour them in.

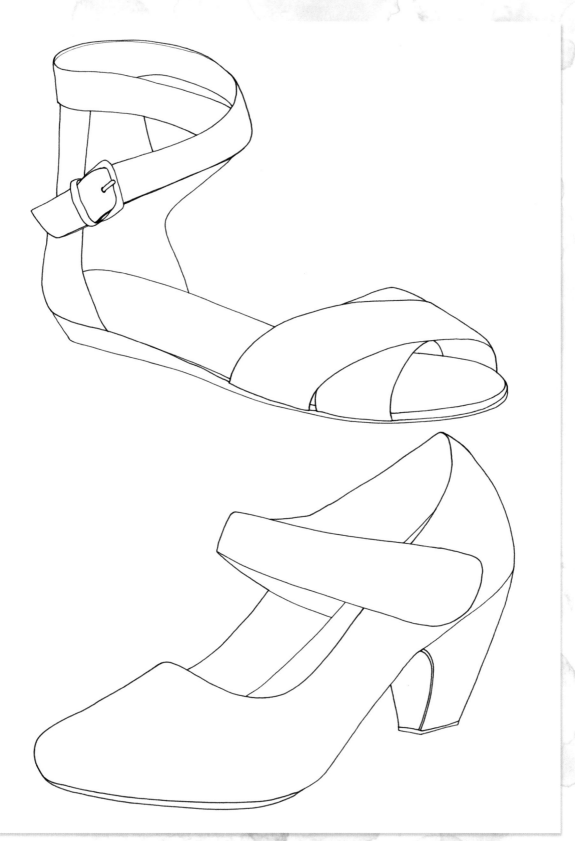

BIRTHDAY WISH LIST

MAKE A LIST BELOW OF EVERYTHING YOU WANT FOR YOUR BIRTHDAY.

☆ ....

☆ ....

☆ ....

☆ ....

☆ ....

☆ ....

☆ ....

☆ ....

☆ ....

☆ ....

☆ ....

☆ ....

You are UNIQUE

I love ...

LIST EVERYTHING YOU LOVE IN YOUR LIFE ON THIS PAGE.

♡ ....

♡ ....

♡ ....

♡ ....

♡ ....

♡ ....

♡ ....

♡ ....

♡ ....

♡ ....

♡ ....

♡ ....

MY FAVOURITE FILMS

LIST ALL YOUR FAVOURITE FILMS BELOW. THERE'S SPACE
TO WRITE A LITTLE REVIEW AND GIVE EACH A SCORE OUT OF TEN.

Film: ....

Reasons I love it: ....

....

....

score: / 10

Film: ....

Reasons I love it: ....

....

....

score: / 10

Film: ....

Reasons I love it: ....

....

....

score: / 10

Film: ....

Reasons I love it: ....

....

....

score: / 10

Film: ....

Reasons I love it: ....

....

....

score: / 10

Film: ....

Reasons I love it: ....

....

....

score: / 10

Film: ....

Reasons I love it: ....

....

....

score: / 10

a great week

WRITE DOWN THE BEST THING THAT
HAPPENED EACH DAY THIS WEEK.

MONDAY: ....

TUESDAY: ....

WEDNESDAY: ....

THURSDAY: ....

FRIDAY: ....

SATURDAY: ....

SUNDAY: ....

PERFECT PARTY

USE THESE PAGES TO WRITE ALL ABOUT A PARTY OR OCCASION YOU HAVE BEEN TO.
WHO ELSE WAS THERE? WHAT DID YOU DO? WAS THERE ANY MUSIC?

Date .... Time .... Place ....

....

....

....

....

....

....

....

....

....

SUMMER HOLIDAY ESSENTIALS

MAKE A LIST BELOW OF ALL YOUR ESSENTIAL SUMMER
HOLIDAY ITEMS, FROM SUN CREAM TO SUNGLASSES.

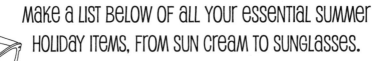

❋ ....

❋ ....

❋ ....

❋ ....

❋ ....

❋ ....

❋ ....

❋ ....

❋ ....

❋ ....

❋ ....

❋ ....

INTERNET SENSATION

HAVE YOU EVER DREAMED OF BECOMING THE NEXT BIG STAR ON THE INTERNET? FILL OUT YOUR ANSWERS BELOW AND DECIDE IF YOU'VE GOT WHAT IT TAKES TO BE A SUCCESSFUL BLOGGER OR VLOGGER.

First things first, what would you call your blog or vlog? You could have a well-known quote in the title or make something brand new up.

....

....

....

....

There are so many things to discuss, what would you focus on? It could be fashion, travel, food and so much more. You might even want to include all of the above!

....

....

....

....

What would your blog look like? Think about colours, pictures and fonts.

....

....

....

....

If you could collaborate with one other internet superstar, who would it be and why?

....

....

....

....

....

....

It's important to focus on the things you are really passionate about. Don't advertise things you don't like and wouldn't use yourself, even if you get paid lots of money to do it. Choose one product you love and write a review below. Think about why you love it, its value for money and why you'd recommend it.

....

....

....

....

....

Now do the same for a product you don't like. Why didn't you like it? Do you think some people might like it more than you? Is there something you would change about the product that you think would make it better?

....

....

....

....

Always be yourself

BEST KEPT SECRETS

USE THIS PAGE TO MAKE A LIST OF THINGS PEOPLE MIGHT NOT KNOW ABOUT YOU. PERHAPS YOU HAVE A SECRET FAVOURITE BAND OR YOU REALLY HATE A CERTAIN TYPE OF FOOD. WRITE DOWN ANYTHING YOU WANT, IT CAN BE TOTALLY RANDOM.

☆ ....

☆ ....

☆ ....

☆ ....

☆ ....

☆ ....

☆ ....

☆ ....

☆ ....

☆ ....

HAPPY HOLIDAYS

USE THESE PAGES TO WRITE ALL ABOUT YOUR SCHOOL HOLIDAYS. WHAT DID YOU GET UP TO? DID YOU MEET UP WITH FRIENDS? DID YOU GO AWAY?

Date .... Time .... Place ....

....

....

....

....

....

....

....

....

....

MY MAKE-UP LOOK BOOK

USE PENS OR PENCILS TO TEST OUT YOUR DREAM MAKE-UP LOOKS ON THESE PAGES.

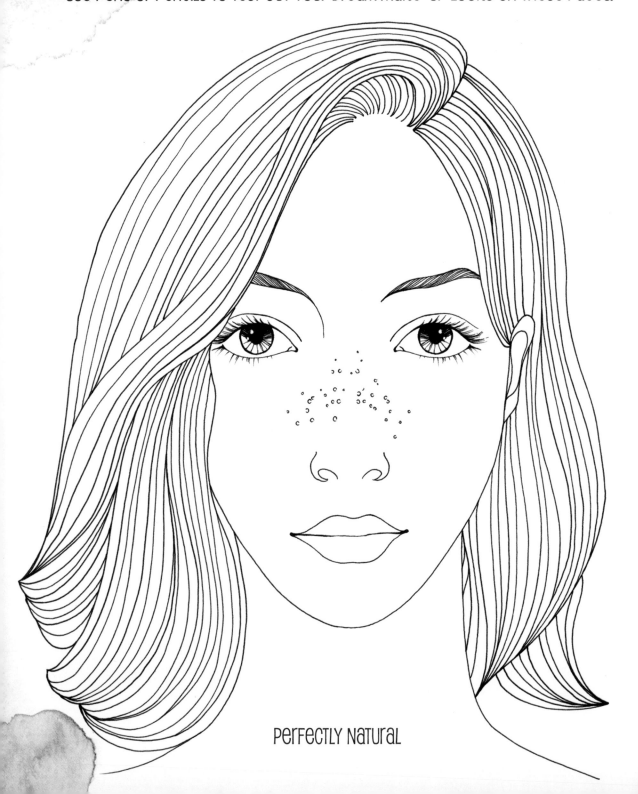

PERFECTLY NATURAL

BOLD & BEAUTIFUL

TOTALLY GLAMOROUS

You are
always
beautiful

PERFECT PLAYLISTS

USE THE SPACES BELOW TO FILL IN YOUR TOP FIVE
SONGS FOR EACH PLAYLIST GENRE. YOU CAN USE
THESE PAGES EVERY TIME YOU NEED SOME INSPIRATION, WHETHER
YOU'RE PLANNING A PARTY OR HAVING A RELAXING EVENING.

PARTY TIME

☆ ....

☆ ....

☆ ....

☆ ....

☆ ....

RELAXATION

❀ ....

❀ ....

❀ ....

❀ ....

❀ ....

CHEESY TUNES

♡ ....

♡ ....

♡ ....

♡ ....

♡ ....

MOVIE SOUNDTRACKS

❀ ....

❀ ....

❀ ....

❀ ....

❀ ....

EMOTIONAL

☆ ....

☆ ....

☆ ....

☆ ....

☆ ....

FUN AND FRIENDS

Here are some top tips for things you could do with your friends. You can use the next page to make a list of everything you do with your friends and add in anything new you want to do with them.

Have a craft afternoon. You could make tie-dye T-shirts, friendship bracelets or paper bunting.

Host an afternoon tea. Get your friends over and make some scones, sandwiches and a pot of tea. Don't forget the cream and jam!

Have a pamper afternoon. Dig out all your favourite nail varnish colours, buy some face masks and get ready to relax.

Arrange a picnic in the park. You can spend all afternoon catching up and eating yummy food.

Have a movie marathon. Choose your favourite films and watch them all in a row. Make sure you have plenty of popcorn to keep you going!

Sleepover! You can watch a good film or box set and eat lots of delicious pizza with your best friends.

♡ ....

♡ ....

♡ ....

♡ ....

♡ ....

♡ ....

♡ ....

♡ ....

♡ ....

♡ ....

♡ ....

♡ ....

♡ ....

Even when
it rains
you can
see a
RAINBOW

DREAM HOLIDAY DESTINATIONS

IF I COULD GO ANYWHERE IN THE WORLD,
I WOULD TRAVEL TO THESE AMAZING PLACES ...

✿ ....

because ....

✿ ....

because ....

✿ ....

because ....

✿ ....

because ....

✿ ....

because ....

✿ ....

because ....

career Day

NOT SURE WHAT YOU WANT TO DO WHEN YOU GROW UP? LOOK THROUGH THESE PERSONALITY TRAITS AND DECIDE WHICH SUITS YOU BEST. USE THE SPACE AT THE END TO WRITE DOWN ANY THOUGHTS OR IDEAS YOU HAVE.

I LOVE WORKING UNDER PRESSURE WITH A TIGHT DEADLINE.

If you can stay calm and collected in stressful situations, you might make a good doctor or lawyer, working in a busy and high-pressured environment.

I PREFER TO WORK AT MY OWN PACE IN A CALM ENVIRONMENT.

Freelance work might suit your mindset. You could work from home or from a studio, perhaps as an illustrator or photographer.

I LIKE TO BE SURROUNDED BY LOTS OF PEOPLE AND CHATTER.

A busy office is the place for you and you might suit a job in a creative industry like design or advertising.

I DON'T WANT TO WORK AT A DESK, I'D RATHER BE OUT AND ABOUT.

If you'd rather have an action-packed job, what about joining the police force or being a sports instructor.

I LIKE MEETING LOTS OF NEW PEOPLE AND WORKING ON DIFFERENT PROJECTS AT THE SAME TIME.

If you would like to get out of the office and meet new clients, a sales representative might be perfect for you, or you may enjoy journalism where you can meet and interview new people all the time.

I LOVE WORKING WITH A LARGE TEAM OF PEOPLE AND I'M NOT AFRAID TO SPEAK UP IN FRONT OF THEM.

You are confident and may have a great stage presence. Perhaps you should consider the performing arts, or you might want to work as a shop manager.

MY THOUGHTS ...

....

....

....

....

....

Beautiful Bags

IT'S YOUR CHANCE TO BE A FASHION DESIGNER. ADD YOUR OWN DOODLES AND DESIGNS TO THESE BAGS, THEN COLOUR THEM IN.

HAPPY THINGS

LIST ALL THE THINGS THAT MAKE YOU HAPPY BELOW. IT COULD BE YOUR BFF, MAYBE IT'S A PET, OR IT COULD JUST BE CHOCOLATE BISCUITS.

☆ ....

☆ ....

☆ ....

☆ ....

☆ ....

☆ ....

☆ ....

☆ ....

☆ ....

☆ ....

☆ ....

Be the reason for someone's smile

WRITE HERE, RIGHT NOW

ANSWER THE QUESTIONS BELOW TO DOCUMENT EXACTLY WHAT IS HAPPENING RIGHT NOW. DON'T FORGET TO ADD THE DATE AND TIME AT THE TOP SO YOU CAN LOOK BACK AND REMEMBER WHEN YOU WROTE THIS.

Date .... Time .... Place ....

Where are you sitting? ....

....

....

What can you see? ....

....

....

Can you smell anything? ....

....

....

What are you wearing? ....

....

....

Are you drinking anything? ....

....

....

Have you got any food? ....

....

....

Are you listening to any music? If so, what is it? ....

....

....

What is the weather like? ....

....

....

Are you with anyone else? ....

....

....

What are you happiest about at this moment in time? ....

....

....

Is anything annoying you right now? ....

....

....

What are you most excited about right now? ....

....

....

MY GREATEST ACHIEVEMENTS

USE THIS SPACE TO WRITE DOWN WHAT YOU'RE REALLY
PROUD OF. YOU CAN KEEP ADDING TO IT OVER TIME SO YOU
ALWAYS REMEMBER WHAT YOU HAVE ACHIEVED.

♡ ....

♡ ....

♡ ....

♡ ....

♡ ....

♡ ....

♡ ....

♡ ....

♡ ....

♡ ....

♡ ....

♡ ....

SILLY SCHOOL STORIES

WRITE DOWN THE FUNNIEST THINGS THAT HAVE EVER HAPPENED AT SCHOOL.

What is the funniest thing that has ever happened in the classroom?

....

....

....

What is the funniest thing that has ever happened in the playground?

....

....

....

What is the silliest thing that has ever happened at lunch? ....

....

....

....

Who is your funniest friend and why? ....

....

....

How many times a day do you laugh at school? ....

....

....

Have you ever laughed so hard that you nearly fell off your chair? ....

....

....

....

Have you or any of your friends ever been told off for laughing so much?

....

....

....

Choose your favourite funny memory and write about it here so you never forget

how much you laughed. ....

....

....

....

Make your DREAMS reality

Beauty Branding

Imagine you have just brought out your very own line of beauty products. Use these templates to design your own gorgeous packaging.

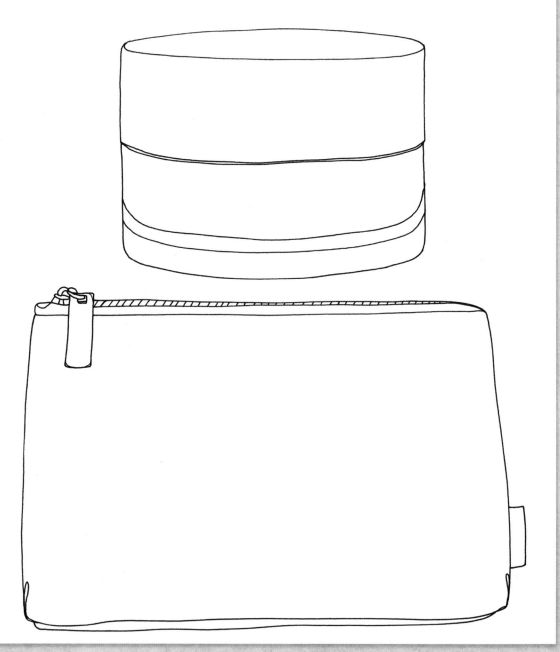

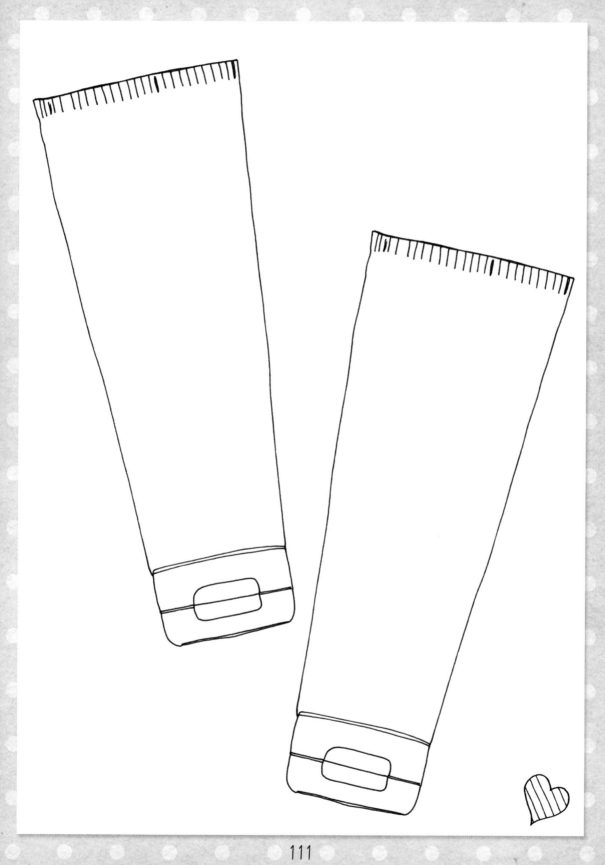

Never give up

FEELING GREAT

EVERYONE FEELS A BIT DOWN IN THE DUMPS OCCASIONALLY,
SO HERE ARE SOME TOP TIPS TO KEEP YOU FEELING POSITIVE.

☆ Surround yourself with the people you love. Your friends and family will always make you smile and you know you can tell them anything that's on your mind.

☆ Do something that makes you happy – anything from watching a film to arranging a shopping trip or listening to music.

☆ Put on your favourite music really loudly and dance around your bedroom!

☆ Don't compare yourself to others. You are unique and that's the best thing you can be.

☆ Do some meditation. You can find lots of videos on YouTube with calming music and breathing instructions that will really help you to relax and feel good about yourself.

☆ Challenge yourself to try something new. It's a great way to meet new people and find new hobbies.

WICKED WEEKEND

Use this space to write all about your weekend.
What did you get up to? Did you see any friends? Did you have fun?

Date .... Time .... Place ....

....

....

....

....

....

....

....

....

....

COSY WINTER ESSENTIALS

Make a list below of all your essential cosy winter items, from scarves to snow boots.

❀ ....

❀ ....

❀ ....

❀ ....

❀ ....

❀ ....

❀ ....

❀ ....

❀ ....

❀ ....

❀ ....

❀ ....

MY FEELINGS

USE THE SPACES BELOW TO RECORD YOUR FEELINGS
AT DIFFERENT TIMES. FILL IN THE DATE AND
TIME FOR EACH ENTRY AS WELL.

Date .... Time ....

TODAY I FEEL .... BECAUSE ....

....

Date .... Time ....

TODAY I FEEL .... BECAUSE ....

....

Date .... Time ....

TODAY I FEEL .... BECAUSE ....

....

Date .... Time ....

TODAY I FEEL .... BECAUSE ....

....

Date ·················· Time ··················

TODAY I FEEL ·························· BECAUSE ··························

··························

Date ·················· Time ··················

TODAY I FEEL ·························· BECAUSE ··························

··························

Date ·················· Time ··················

TODAY I FEEL ·························· BECAUSE ··························

··························

Date ·················· Time ··················

TODAY I FEEL ·························· BECAUSE ··························

··························

Date ·················· Time ··················

TODAY I FEEL ·························· BECAUSE ··························

··························

SCHOOL SURVEY

answer all the questions below to keep a record of your school experience, right here, right now. you can look back at this in the future and remember everything about your school.

Date .... Time .... Place ....

What is your school called? ....

....

What year are you in? ....

....

Who are your best friends? ....

....

Who is your favourite teacher? ....

....

Who is your least favourite teacher? ....

....

What are your favourite subjects? ....

....

....

If you could drop one subject what would it be? ....

....

....

Describe your school uniform. Do you love it or hate it? ....

....

....

What do you hate the most about school? ....

....

....

What is your favourite thing about school? ....

....

....

Rate your school out of 10: | / 10 |

Make
every
moment
count

MY FAVOURITE SONGS

ADD ALL YOUR FAVOURITE SONGS TO THE LIST BELOW.

SONG: .... by ....

SONG: .... by ....

SONG: .... by ....

SONG: .... by ....

SONG: .... by ....

SONG: .... by ....

SONG: .... by ....

SONG: .... by ....

SONG: .... by ....

SONG: .... by ....

SONG: .... by ....

SONG: .... by ....

ACTS OF KINDNESS

THIS YEAR, WHY NOT TRY TO DO ONE GOOD DEED EACH MONTH. THERE ARE 12 SPACES BELOW FOR YOU TO FILL IN THE DETAILS OF EACH OCCASION. YOU COULD DONATE OLD CLOTHES AND BOOKS TO A CHARITY SHOP, HAVE A BAKE SALE TO RAISE MONEY FOR CHARITY OR HELP OUT YOUR PARENTS AROUND THE HOUSE.

JANUARY ....

....

FEBRUARY ....

....

MARCH ....

....

APRIL ....

....

MAY ....

....

JUNE ....

....

JULY ....

....

AUGUST ....

....

SEPTEMBER ....

....

OCTOBER ....

....

NOVEMBER ....

....

DECEMBER ....

....

SUPER SCHOOL DAY

USE THESE PAGES TO WRITE ALL ABOUT YOUR DAY AT SCHOOL. WHAT DID YOU DO? DID ANYTHING FUNNY HAPPEN? DID YOU HANG OUT WITH ANY FRIENDS?

Date .... Time .... Place ....

....

....

....

....

....

....

....

....

....